THE KINDNESS BOOK

TODD PARR

Megan Tingley Books

LITTLE, BROWN AND COMPANY

NEW YORK BOSTON

For Tammy

About This Book

The illustrations for this book were created on a drawing tablet using an iMac, starting with bold black lines and dropping in color with Adobe Photoshop. This book was edited by Megan Tingley and Anna Prendella and designed by Saho Fujii. The production was supervised by Erika Breglia, and the production editor was Marisa Finkelstein. The text was set in Todd Parr's signature font.

Copyright © 2019 by Todd Parr • Cover illustration copyright © 2019 by Todd Parr. Cover design by Saho Fujii. • Cover copyright © 2019 by Hachette Book Group, Inc. • Hachette Book Group supports the right to free expression and the value of copyright. The purpose of copyright is to encourage writers and artists to produce the creative works that enrich our culture. • The scanning, uploading, and distribution of this book without permission is a theft of the author's intellectual property. If you would like permission to use material from the book (other than for review purposes), please contact permissions@hbgusa.com. Thank you for your support of the author's rights. • Little, Brown and Company • Hachette Book Group • 1290 Avenue of the Americas, New York, NY 10104 • Visit us at LBYR.com • First Edition: October 2019 • Little, Brown and Company is a division of Hachette Book Group, Inc. The Little, Brown name and logo are trademarks of Hachette Book Group, Inc. • The publisher is not responsible for websites (or their content) that are not owned by the publisher. Library of Congress Cataloging-in-Publication Data • Names: Parr, Todd, author. • Title: The kindness book / Todd Parr. • Description: First Edition. | New York: Little, Brown and Company, 2019. | "Megan Tingley books." • Identifiers: LCCN 2019007075| ISBN 9780316423816 (hardcover) | ISBN 9780316533980 (ebook) | ISBN 9780316534116 (library edition ebook) Subjects: LCSH: Kindness—Juvenile literature. • Classification: LCC BJ1533.K5 P37 2019 | DDC 177/.7—dc23 • LC record available at https://lccn.loc.gov/2019007075 • ISBNs: 978-0-316-42381-6 (hardcover), 978-0-316-53412-3 (ebook), 978-0-316-53391-1 (ebook), 978-0-316-53398-0 (ebook) • PRINTED IN CHINA • APS • 10 9 8 7 6 5 4 3 2 1

Kindness is thinking about people's
feelings and helping them feel good.
Being kind makes you feel good, too!

Kindness is reading a bedtime story to someone you love.

Kindness is taking care of your community.

Kindness is holding the door open for someone.

Kindness is listening.

Kindness is keeping others safe.

KIN

IS

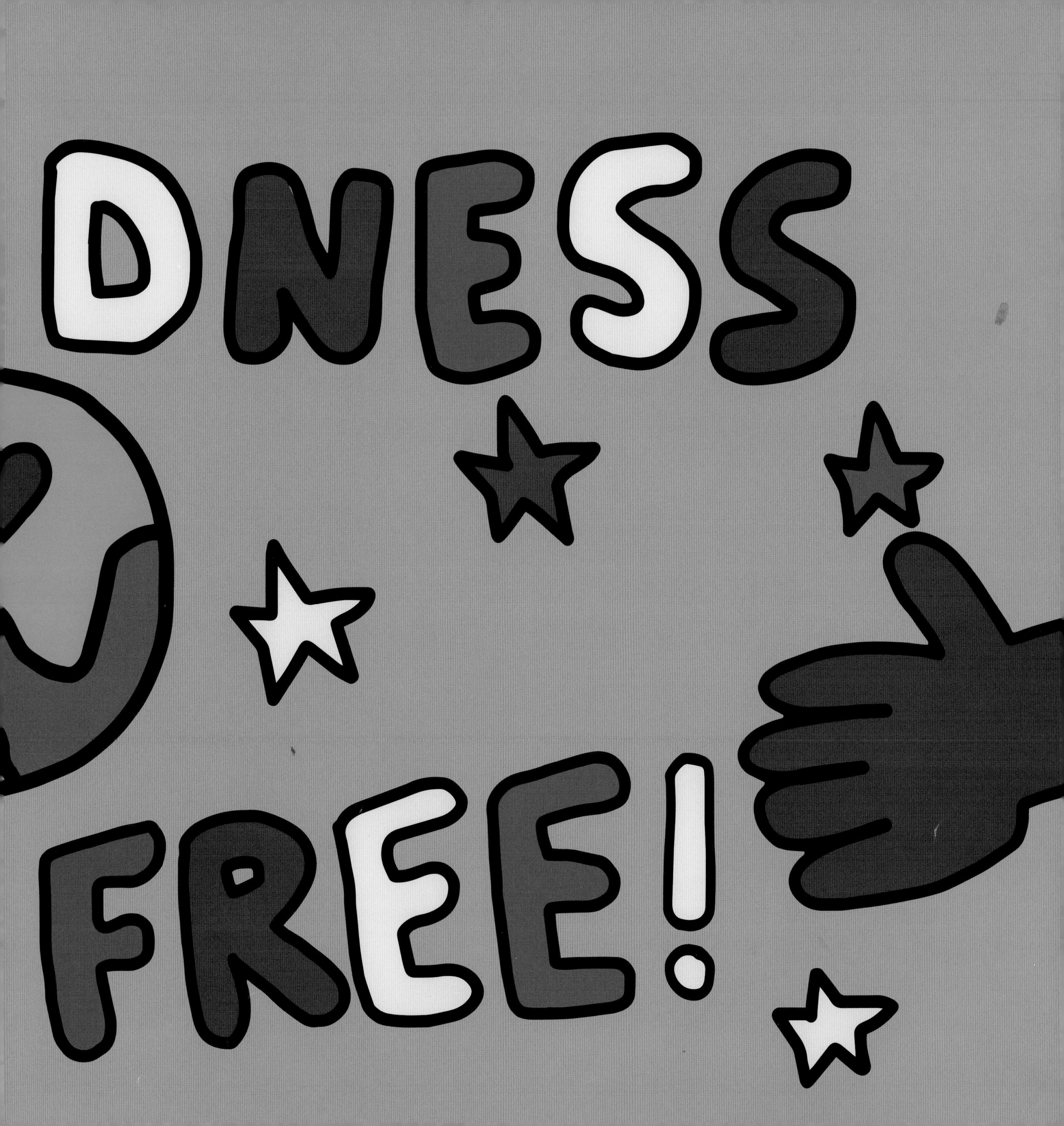
DNESS
FREE!

Kindness is watching out for
someone around you.

Kindness is holding hands.

Kindness is being there when someone needs you.

Kindness is taking care of yourself.

Kindness is helping things grow.

Kindness is saying something nice.

Kindness is not hurting someone's feelings.

Kindness is saying sorry.

Kindness is remembering everyone's feelings are important.

Kindness is welcoming someone
new to the family.

Kindness is giving a bug a hug.

Kindness is saying hello to someone new.

Kindness is saying thank you to those who help others.

Kindness is being nice to animals.

Kindness is letting others be who they are.

Kindness is cheering someone up
when they are sad.

IT'S
EASY TO
BE
KIND!

There are many ways to be kind! Don't forget to be kind to YOURSELF.

The end. LOVE, Todd

KINDNESS IS FREE